The Tale of the Cat with the Crooked Tail

By

Maureen Julie McGrath

Strategic Book Publishing and Rights Co.

Happy Birthday! Merry Christmas!, just "The Elf on the shelf said you were good"! Keep reading You'll love it! Maureen & Giggles '2021

Strategic Book Publishing and Rights Co.
12620 FM 1960, Suite A4-507
Houston, TX 77065
www.sbpra.com

ISBN: 978-1-62516-859-7

To those who have been bullied: You are beautiful and loved

Acknowledgment

To those special people in my life who never gave up on me.

And to Mark for your encouragement with my writing.

This is the tale of a cat

A special cat at that

But there was one difference in this cute male

He had what you would call a
crooked tail

She called him Giggles, because he made her smile

He was a special friend to her for awhile

Zigzag , unstraight, or funny you may say

This cat was special in so many ways

Giggles had friends—Mattie, Precious, and Blacky

They laughed at his tail and thought it was wacky

The alley cats would tease him

And make him feel alone

He felt so sad and lonely

All he wanted to be was home

He knew he was loved and his friends
would never fail

To play with the cat with the crooked tail

CPSIA information can be obtained
at www.ICGtesting.com
Printed in the USA
LVHW020722241021
701355LV00001B/4